Nick Jr.

DORA the EXPLORER

W9-CBE-657

Eggs for Everyone!

by Laura Driscoll
illustrated by A&J Studios

Ready-to-Read

Simon Spotlight/Nick Jr.

New York   London   Toronto   Sydney

Based on the TV series *Dora the Explorer*® as seen on Nick Jr.®

SIMON SPOTLIGHT
An imprint of Simon & Schuster Children's Publishing Division
1230 Avenue of the Americas
New York, New York 10020
Copyright © 2005 Viacom International Inc. All rights reserved.
NICKELODEON, NICK JR., *Dora the Explorer,* and all related titles, logos, and characters
are registered trademarks of Viacom International Inc.
All rights reserved, including the right of reproduction in whole or in part in any form.
READY-TO-READ, SIMON SPOTLIGHT, and colophon are
registered trademarks of Simon & Schuster, Inc.
Manufactured in the United States of America
4 6 8 10 9 7 5
Library of Congress Cataloging-in-Publication Data
Driscoll, Laura.
Eggs for everyone! / by Laura Driscoll ; illustrated by A&J Studios.— 1st ed.
p. cm. — (Dora the explorer ready-to-read ; #7)
"Based on the TV series Dora the Explorer as seen on Nick Jr."—T.p.
Summary: Dora and her friend Boots decorate eggs for their families and friends.
ISBN 0-689-87176-7
[1. Egg decoration—Fiction.] I. A&J Studios. II. Title.
III. Ready-to-read. Level 1, Dora the explorer ; #7.
PZ7.D79Eg 2005
[E]—dc22
2004004969

Hi! I am .

DORA

and I are coloring

BOOTS

for our friends.

EGGS

We are making  BLUE EGGS

and YELLOW EGGS and

PINK EGGS and ORANGE EGGS .

We put stickers

on some  EGGS .

We have stickers of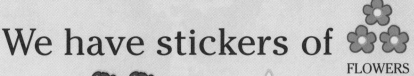

FLOWERS

and  and

TEDDY BEARS   STARS

and other things too.

Now we can take the **EGGS**

to our friends!

There is .

loves .

Do you know which

we made for ?

Look! It is  's
BOOTS

mommy and daddy.

They live with
BOOTS

in a .
TREE HOUSE

Which  did  make for them?

EGG   BOOTS

TICO likes to drive
his little YELLOW CAR.
Which EGG
did we make for TICO?

 loves  .

DIEGO   BABY JAGUAR

Which  did we make

EGG

for  ?

DIEGO

I love my  and .
The  I made them
shows how much.

MAMI PAPI EGG

Which ⬭ EGG is for 🧍 and 🧍? MAMI PAPI

BENNY loves TEDDY BEARS.

BENNY TEDDY BEARS

Which EGG did we make

EGG

for BENNY?

BENNY

 is a

⭐ catcher

just like me.

Which  EGG

is for ? ABUELA

Oh, look!

There is one  left
EGG

in the .
BASKET

Who is it for?

Need a hint? and I made this

BOOTS   EGG

for someone who

helped us today.

BOOTS and I made this  EGG

for you!

We hope you like it!